City
of
Mazes

Cynthia Hendershot

CITY OF
MAZES

AND OTHER TALES OF OBSESSION

Santa Maria
ASYLUM ARTS
1993

Acknowledgements

The author wishes to express thanks to the editors of the following magazines, in which some of these stories first appeared: *Asylum Annual, Bakunin, Blank Gun Silencer, Schmaga, Shattered Wig Review*.

ISBN 1-878580-41-8
Library of Congress Catalogue Number: 93-70303

Printed in the United States of America.

The publication of this book was funded in part by a Gregory Kolovakos Seed Grant administered by the Coordinating Council of Literary Magazines and Small Presses (CLMP).

Contents

City of Mazes

Seven Days

The first day I found fingers in the envelope. Four smooth glass fingers arrived safely, but your letter was broken. It shattered on the way. I cut my hand on slivers of your words.

*

The second day you sent me a sigh frozen in a black glass. When I opened the box it melted to blue smoke and floated to the ceiling. A single drop of blood fell on my palm.

*

The third day I touched your amputated heart. I unwrapped the silver paper and gently stroked it. All day I sucked my blood-stained fingers. It was like tasting you.

*

The fourth day you sent me the web of your silence. Fragmented words struggled hopelessly against invisible spiders. I sat still and ran my fingers across my throat.

*

The fifth day my eyes filled with green fog. I could only feel what you sent me, the supple curve of a night of red lightening and sweat. I breathed in your deep body scent.

*

The sixth day my body was ice. You sent me an ice pick made of black pearl and I stabbed my chest until small drops of blood fell down my belly like tears.

*

The seventh day the sky cracked open and your body slid through the crevices of broken clouds. I reached out to you, passion squirming through my hair like black and red snakes.

The Passion

You are in every room of the house. I know. I walk through it every day with tourists who come to see projected images of your pain. Everyone's interested since you disappeared that June evening. Your house has become a museum, a shrine. I tour it every day looking for you inside the walls, sliding my hands up and down the projected images of you.

My favorite room is the Crucifixion Room. That's what they call it now, though it used to be the bedroom, the bedroom where we made love, the bedroom where I gently caressed every part of your body, the bedroom where we sucked and ate each other like ripe cherries.

Now your image lies naked on a white bedspread. The bed is so neat it hurts my eyes. They've taken away the tangled sheets where we used to lie together Sunday mornings talking and laughing and making love until our skin was raw. Now your image lies naked on that immaculate white bedspread with bleeding palms and clear blue eyes fixed in an ecstasy of suffering. They've taken the books and furniture away to make the room look like a monk's cell. They've made you into a saint.

When you slipped out of my arms that day my body went numb. They asked me questions but all I could say was that there was a passionate light in your eyes, then you slipped away. I could smell you on my clothes and body, but you were gone.

Now all my days revolve around that final image of you. We are standing on the sidewalk embracing. The last rays of sun are flickering on a parking meter. Suddenly I'm no longer aware of our surroundings. I'm staring into your deep brown eyes and there is this incredible red light pouring out of them. It's like seeing an emotion, seeing passion. Then you disappear. I reach out for you, then sink down onto the sidewalk. There are crowds of people around me asking questions. They put me in an ambulance. I think I feel your hot breath on my neck, but it's only a fever enveloping me like a black cloak.

I was sick for a long time. All the lights went out in my brain and everything turned black. Then one day as I was sitting on the edge of my hospital bed I saw a discarded red ribbon in a corner of the room. It looked so fragile. I was sure you had left it there for me. Then I saw myself in your house. I saw all those days we spent there compressed into a single image, the image of me standing naked at the window looking at a full moon while you walk up behind me and slowly slide your arms around my waist. All the windows fly open and the whole house glows like lava.

Now they've turned your house into a shrine. They burned all your things and make everything white. One night while they were vandalizing your house I broke in and stole an old sweater and your ashtrays. They had left one old brown sweater on a hanger. I felt a knife slit my heart when I saw it in the empty closet. I stuffed it in my bag. I took two ashtrays filled with your cigarette butts and carefully wrapped them in my coat. This is all I have left of you.

City of Mazes

I keep getting lost in a tunnel. I stumble, grasp at the curtains, then fall, bruising my knees and hand. Veins swell and I'm sure they'll explode, but they only turn purple.

There is so much passion in my veins. I've moved to a city of mazes where I lose myself every night in a different room. I move through this city like I used to move through your interior, only now I'm cold.

At first I couldn't feel anything. I thought I was losing my heart to a bandit who would sell it in the silver courtyard of the city of mazes, but when I ripped the mask from his eyes, I saw the bandit was you. I couldn't comprehend that you were stealing part of my body. I sat still with my blouse unbuttoned.

Later I washed the blood off my breasts and caressed them gently like you used to do. I looked at my face in the mirror. I thought that the woman in the mirror was suffering, her face was pale, her brow was wrinkled, but I couldn't see that the woman was me.

Then one night I woke up tangled in the sheets. I was trying to strangle myself with sheets that still smelled of your body. I got up, broke every glass in my apartment, and ran naked into the street screaming your name. That's when they put me in the city of mazes.

I remember all those gray faces asking me questions I couldn't hear. I thought they all had cotton in their mouths. I grabbed one of their guns and shot myself in the hand. I watched my blood gush onto the black checkered floor, but I couldn't feel anything. The next morning as I was being questioned I stuck a pencil into the gray hand of the police chief. He cried out in pain. I laughed, ripped off my bandage and began sucking my wound.

The next thing I remember is waking up in the city of mazes where women wear necklaces made of sparrow bones and old discarded lovers peer from chiaroscuro lighted apartments. They sent me here to look for you.

They said I lost control because you amputated my heart. They said you did it gently, like a surgeon. They said I was lucky. It could have been a bloody, painful experience.

Every night I walk through streets and tunnels and rooms looking for you.

Once I heard your laughter in a café filled with blind men. I walked in the door of the white building, glancing at the black mirrors that decorated the walls, but you had gone.

I know you had been there. There were five red feathers on the floor, five red feathers that resembled passion.

One night I heard a deep-voiced woman call out your name as she reached orgasm. I ran up three flights of stairs to her one room apartment and saw your cigarette burning in her marble ashtray. She pulled the sheet over her plump body and smiled lewdly at me.

I live in a two-room apartment in the city of mazes, an apartment with black walls and green venetian blinds. I've decorated the walls with enlarged photographs of every part of your body. Your left ear hangs in the bathroom. Your penis hangs at the foot of my bed.

I never bother looking for you in the daytime. I know you're sleeping somewhere, in some dingy room. I know my heart is hidden in the closet under your dirty trousers and shirts. I know I can never find this room.

But at night you roam the streets looking for women. You said you loved women most before making love to them. You live for the moment of anticipation before you make a new conquest. Many times you described the precise expression on my face and the light in my eyes that golden moment before you pulled me on top of you.

I know one night I will find you in the arms of one these phantom women who haunt the city of mazes. I will find you sweating, exposed, red light covering your naked flesh. I will find you and I will cut out your heart with a pearl knife. I will place your heart in the hole in my chest. I will laugh as shadows fall across your face and you realize that now you must roam lonely streets at night. Now you must stumble through tunnels and empty rooms in search of your amputated heart.

Glass

I spread my hand across the window, caress the place where your ass is pressed. I watch your closed eyes in the mirror as you stand fucking her, her thin body draped over the bed, her hands clenching the black bedspread like clumps of flesh. I watch smiling, my lids heavy, my eyes blazing. I watch but you don't see me, only a flash of teeth as I crouch in the bushes.

The next day I leave a message on your answering machine: I'm going to kill you. I sit on my bed, imagine your face turning white, imagine her eyes widening. I dig my nails into my palm.

The next evening I am sitting in a restaurant smoking cigarette after cigarette. I see you come in with her. You look tired and thin, a luminous mummy in a black suit. She clings to your arm, all red hair and black lace stockings. I shatter a wine glass in my hand.

My bleeding hand wrapped in a napkin, I watch the two of you eat. You talk, run your fingers through your black hair, stare at her breasts as she penetrates you with her eyes.

Under the table I'm holding a knife. I begin carving the underside of the table, fantasizing it is your ass. I see pearls of blood rolling off your soft white flesh.

The next day I leave another message on your machine: I want you to make me come before I kill you. It is late and I am walking around your neighborhood, hoping to hear your voice, the echo of your footsteps. I lower my head, shielding my cigarette from the wind. I reach for matches in my pocket. You tap my shoulder, take my cigarette, light it in your mouth, give it back to me. My hand is shaking too much to smoke. I crush the cigarette with the black and silver toe of my shoe.

You take my hand, lead me to your house, undress me, wrap me in your trenchcoat. You fall to your knees, your snake eyes shimmering in the mirror. I watch you kiss my thighs, stroke my belly, tie my hands behind my back. You drape me across the bed, turn your back to the window.

I wake up sweating. These dreams of you gnaw inside with razor teeth. I wash my face, decide to phone you. This time she answers. Her voice oozes into my ear, I slam down the phone. I pace up and down the room, trying to stop the sickness rising in my belly. I reach for a bottle, drink.

At 2 a.m. I am lying on the floor, wearing your old sweater, fondling photographs of your face and body. I change clothes, put on black lace stockings and a red wig. I begin walking toward your house. I stand watching her twisted face, your thrusting body. Your eyes are closed, you smile, crooked teeth jut from your lips like broken rocks. I watch. I become excited by the outlines of your body, the tufts of hair under your armpits, the scar on your belly. I start to cry out for you, then stop myself by biting my lip. I clasp my pearl necklace. It breaks, pearls scatter across the dark sidewalk.

I slam my fist through the window, clasp a shard of glass which slices my hand. I raise the shard above your ass. Our dark eyes meet in the mirror.

Murder

I look for my reflection in the pool of blood lying next to your body. I see only brief flashes of eyes, quivering flesh, outstretched hands. I lie on top of your dead body, stroke your hair, gently kiss your neck. The perfume of your murderer lingers in the room. I cover your eyes with black lace panties and go looking for her, the woman who shot you.

Smell of sweat, blood, cigarettes in the small room where I wait. Faceless bodies of prostitutes positioned like marble statues. Suddenly my hands tremble. I think of you holding me, you pulling me onto a black bed where red feathers sprout on our naked bodies, closed eyes, hands opening me, silk fingers, echoed sighs. I light a cigarette and bite my knuckles.

A blonde woman wearing a tight black dress calls me into an office where posters of naked women drown me as I sit on an overstuffed pink couch. I show her the photograph of your murderer. She looks at it, returns it to me, pats me on the hand. I stare at a photograph of an empty white room. Your murderer has vanished from the snapshot.

I leave quickly, bump into a red-head wearing nothing but fishnet stockings. She touches me on the ass. Outside I feel faint. I stumble to the nearest café and order a carafe of red wine. I can almost feel your breath on my neck as I drink a third glass of wine. I fight images of your naked body which flutter before me, then I grasp them, drink them more greedily than I do the wine. Faces in hotel mirrors, clasped hands, tangled sheets, blue rings of smoke spiraling to the ceiling.

A waitress hands me a pink envelope. Inside I find a note: I must see you. You must know. I want to feel you close to me. I crumple up the note in my hand, dig my nails into my palm. I think of her black eyes watching me now, pinning me to the chair, pulling me apart, piece by piece.

You stand before me holding the gun that killed you. You beckon me. I move toward you, try to touch you, but you disappear in a cloud of black smoke. I fall to the ground, call out your name. When I look up she is holding the gun above my head. She gives it to me. I stick the barrel in my mouth. She begins undressing. She wraps her fishnet stockings around my neck, kisses me on the cheek, moves my finger close to the trigger. As I squeeze the trigger she smiles lewdly.

I awake from the dream shaking. I reach out to you across the bed, grasp cold air. I pull the blankets close to me, sniff them, try to smell traces of your body. I haven't changed the bedclothes since you were killed. I keep your cigarette butts in an envelope beneath my pillow.

I am waiting for her. I sit in a crowded restaurant filled with emaciated lovers and dark-eyed waiters. I see her moving toward my table. She is dressed completely in black. She smiles at me, runs her long white fingers through her hair.

I pour her a glass of wine, averting her stare. I light a cigarette with a trembling hand. Blood rushes to my face. My hand reaches for the knife. I want to kill her. I want to see her body surrounded by a pool of blood. I want to touch her cold flesh like I touched yours. I want to lie between your body and hers as I turn into an ice statue.

We don't speak. As she pours herself another glass of wine I feel her foot moving up my leg. I stand, move toward the exit.

Outside the restaurant I am paralyzed. Cold air pierces my lungs. I sink to the ground, ripped by your image. I see your body reflected in a hall of mirrors. I stumble through glass walls in search of you. You touch my bleeding body with a gloved hand. I embrace you, smearing your white flesh with red. We fall to the ground, grind our bodies on shattered mirrors.

She leads me to her apartment. I sit on her couch shaking. She hands me a letter, a letter in your handwriting. I open it, try to read the words but they evaporate. I stare at a blank piece of paper.

She leads me into her bedroom. In the candle-lit room I see your corpse spread across her bed. I move toward you. She grabs me, pushes me against the wall, ties my hands with a black leather strap, kisses me hard in the mouth.

She takes off her clothes, spreads them across your body, black leather skirt, fishnet stockings, silk panties. Then she removes her mask and walks toward me. I stand frozen, my eyes closed. She kisses me again and leaves. I watch her walk slowly down a dim-lit sidewalk, watch her fade into black night.

I wake up next to your cold body.

Silence

You pull back the black velvet curtains and I am lying there naked, bound to the bed with black leather ropes which cut into my ankles and wrists. You sit on the edge of the bed and gently stroke my calves. You kiss me lightly on the lips and leave.

*

The next morning I sit at a café table smoking, my black wool skirt presses close to my thighs. You walk up behind me and tie a red scarf around my neck. I reach up to stroke your cheek, but you have vanished. A raven's feather hovers in midair.

*

It is a red room where I see you sitting naked except for a black and white polka-dotted tie which dangles from your neck. A thin woman dressed in black lace feeds you thick slices of roast beef from a silver plate. She teases your mouth with the rare meat. Blood and grease drip on your tie as I stare at your beautiful erection.

*

I stand outside your window. I wear a black leather trenchcoat with nothing underneath. I stare at the pale blue light behind your white lace curtains. My thighs tremble as I write my name in lipstick on your sidewalk.

*

My room is filled with fog. It floats over the bed and envelopes my legs. It smells like you, like your body, like the crevices where you hide dark veins which quiver at the slightest touch. I imagine your naked body transformed into a single vein, I see my hands caressing it as it throbs purple and red.

*

My black fishnet stockinged legs slide along the bedpost. I see your dark face peering from beneath the sheets. I look at you, eyes open, back arched. You kiss my inner thigh as you fade to black.

*

Hands on my breasts gently stroking, a tongue licking my earlobe, and my hands searching, grasping flesh, pushing it into my bleeding pores. I kiss your eyelids as you enter me.

*

When you've gone silence drips down my thighs like blood.

Feet

Charlotte kisses her lover's white foot, runs her tongue along the blue veins, rubs her lips against the tufts of black hair. Her lover moans. Charlotte slowly moves her hands up his legs and begins unfastening his belt.

"No," he whispers. "Just the foot. Suck the toes." Charlotte sucks his long thin toes. She becomes more and more excited.

Her lover continues to moan. He cries out her name, his body thrashes. He reaches orgasm and pulls Charlotte up off the floor, kisses her hard on the mouth. She thrills at the touch of his tongue and teeth.

Overcome with passion she says, "Julian, I love you."

"Yes, darling, and I love your feet." Julian grabs Charlotte's size-seven foot and begins caressing it. "Focus all of your being into your foot," he whispers. Charlotte concentrates. Slowly Julian's black and white living room fades. Charlotte feels a throbbing in her foot. She is swimming in a black sea of foam. Fish slither between her thighs. Red shafts of light shoot into her. When she surfaces, Julian is laughing.

"Charlotte, you came!"

"Yes," she sighs, running her fingers through her short black hair. "It's very odd." Julian and Charlotte go to lunch. They sit intoxicated by the wine and the after shocks of their erotic morning. Julian is dressed entirely in black. On one white finger a band of rubies shimmers. His eyes are sunken and dark. He lights a cigarette.

Charlotte touches him lightly on the hand. "Julian, are you feeling okay?"

"Yes, I was just wondering . . ."

"Yes?"

"Well, if it's enough for you."

Charlotte leans over the table and kisses him on the cheek. "Yes," she whispers.

But Julian is no longer paying attention to Charlotte; he is captivated by the small feet of a statuesque blonde who has just entered the restaurant. Her feet, clad in four-inch black heels, cause him to get an erection. He quickly looks away from the woman and clasps Charlotte's hand. He places her hand in his lap.

Charlotte smiles. They both stand and move toward the women's bathroom. They lock themselves inside. Charlotte removes Julian's foot from his black leather shoe, then peels his argyle sock off with her teeth. Outside a woman rattles the door handle. "Just a minute," Julian shouts.

Julian buys Charlotte an ankle bracelet for her birthday and asks her to move in with him.

When she brings her things to Julian's black and white house, he gives her a set of keys. "Why so many?" she asks.

"I'm a very private person."

On their first night of cohabitation, Charlotte emerges from the bathroom wearing only the red ruby ankle bracelet Julian gave her. Julian, lying in bed wearing black silk pajamas, jumps up, and leads her to a black chair he has placed in the center of the bedroom.

"Sit here," he says. "I want to look at your feet." Charlotte complies. "Thrust them out. . . yes . . ." Julian lies on the floor gazing at her white feet, the supple curves of her toes, the violence of the red polish carefully covering the nails.

In the morning Charlotte awakens in the chair. Her feet have been tied together with Julian's pajama top. Julian lies sprawled on the floor, naked and smiling.

As he leaves for work, Julian kisses her naked feet. "See you tonight."

Charlotte has the entire day free. Her work doesn't resume for another week. She decides to spend the day exploring the house.

An immense structure, decorated entirely in black and white art deco, the house excites Charlotte. She hopes to discover some key to Julian's personality. She searches through desk drawers, closets, but to her dismay, she finds nothing. Everything is orderly. The house is impersonal, antiseptic.

Depressed, Charlotte sits down to have lunch at the black kitchen table. She notices a closet in the kitchen which she hasn't explored. Leaving her pasta salad untouched, she tries to open the door. None of the keys works.

Julian arrives home with a bouquet of black roses. His eyes seem darker and his face paler. In his hand he holds a black shopping bag. Charlotte takes the flowers from him.

"Thank you." She kisses him lightly on the mouth. "What's in the bag?"

"Oh, nothing, something for the antique shop. Shall I make us dinner?"

"Marvelous." Charlotte places her foot on the white coffee table. "But first..."

"One moment, darling." Julian kisses her deeply on the mouth until she feels lightheaded. Her foot begins to throb. Julian goes into the kitchen. She hears him open a door, then close it. He returns without the shopping bag. Then he removes his clothes and peels Charlotte's stockings off. She moans as he sucks her big toe. She falls back onto the coffee table, knocking over a black vase which shatters on the white tiled floor. Julian, who is thrashing on the he floor, slices his knee on one of the slivers.

After she comes, Charlotte gasps when she sees Julian's blood flowing onto the white tiles. Julian smiles. "Sexy, isn't it?" He smears his blood on her big toe. Charlotte stares into his dark eyes. For the first time, she feels frightened of him. As they are eating their swordfish, she asks him about the closet. "I just wondered," she says, "because I wanted to store some things there. Dishes, you know."

"Oh," Julian says, running his fingers through his hair. "It's full. Packed with things of mine."

"Okay." Charlotte feels her curiosity burn inside like a flaming coal. I must see what's there, she thinks. She pours herself another glass of wine as Julian lights a cigarette.

That night Charlotte dreams she is blindfolded. Julian leads her to the closet. Inside she sees herself impaled on a metal spike. Her blood flows onto the white tiles and stains them with the imprints of rose petals. Charlotte awakens, reaches out for Julian, but finds he is gone.

She stand up, dazed by the dream, and begins searching for Julian. The house is extremely quiet. She hears a low chanting which appears to be coming from the kitchen. She clenches her hands and moves toward the sound.

As she is about to turn the corner which leads to the kitchen, she hears keys jangling. She crouches down beside the sofa as Julian emerges from the kitchen. In the moonlit room, Charlotte catches a brief glimpse of his face. His hair is ruffled, his pajamas are disordered, and his eyes are sunken into their sockets.

Ice water flows through Charlotte's veins. She digs her nails into her palm until a single drop of blood drips down her wrist and falls onto the white tiled floor. When she returns to the bedroom, Julian is sitting on the edge of the bed waiting for her. He looks at her with blazing eyes, yet his voice is calm.

"Where have you been?"

"Sorry, I couldn't sleep." Charlotte bites at a hangnail.

"Where did you go?" Julian speaks in a low monotonous voice.

"Well, I just walked around the house a bit."

Julian stands and grabs Charlotte by the wrist. She makes a soft cry of protest. "Like the kitchen, for example?" Charlotte shakes her head. She is too frightened to speak. Julian's dark eyes are smothering her. She finds it difficult to breathe.

Julian pushes her onto the bed and rips her black nightgown to shreds. Then he removes two black leather cords from the bedside table. He binds her feet together, then her hands. Charlotte is too dazed to struggle. She lies there passively waiting. Julian stares at her. Suddenly she is no longer frightened, just aroused.

Julian kisses her on the mouth, bites her ear, her neck. Charlotte's excitement mounts. Then Julian climbs on top of her and enters her.

She feels as if her bones will break. Her cries echo through the quiet house like steel spikes shattering glass. She is falling to the bottom of an endless gorge. Brambles scratch her face, sharp rocks gouge her belly.

Charlotte awakens with limbs unbound. Julian is gone. She sits up, feeling drained. The pleasure and the pain of the night blur, black and red lines severing her brain into small pieces.

She puts on Julian's pajama top and reaches for her watch on the bedside table. She feels a set of keys there, Julian's keys. She picks them up and notices a red spot on one of them. She examines the key. It's a blood stain. She lies back on the bed. She knows Julian left the keys there for her. Her body freezes.

Charlotte sits in the kitchen slowly drinking a cup of coffee. She stares at the keys shining on the black table. She remembers Julian's warm flesh inside her. She thinks of his pale face and the dark bags under his eyes. She imagines him dead. She thinks of his black and white corpse spread out on the white kitchen table. He would make a beautiful corpse, she thinks, then laughs nervously.

She fondles the blood-stained key, places it in her mouth, licks the metallic blood. Then very slowly she moves toward the closet door. She opens the door, goes inside, closes it behind her.

She fumbles in the dark for the light. Overwhelmed by the stench of the room, she must steady herself. She reaches out and touches something cold. Her fingers explore it. Finally, her hand finds the pull cord for the overhead light. The naked bulb illuminates the object she is fondling, a severed foot with red lacquered toenails. She picks it up, explores it. The gore is still fresh at the top. Black blood stains her fingers.

Her head begins to spin. She struggles to see the rest of the room. There are severed feet throughout the closet, poised on black and white stands like statues. All women's feet, slender, white, with red nails. She sits in the middle of the floor, stares at her own feet.

The door begins to open slowly . She looks up at Julian as he enters the room carrying a butcher knife. She stares into his dark eyes.

"I love you, Julian," she whispers.

"I know," he says, moving toward her. As she extends her foot toward him, the red ruby ankle bracelet glimmers in the pale light. Julian delicately removes it, places it in his pocket, then bends down and gently kisses each toe.

"I love you too," Julian says, as he positions Charlotte's foot on the floor and raises the butcher knife.

Playground

In a dark, abandoned playground a woman stands clutching a black coat to her thin body, fighting the wind which stirs up candy wrappers, torn letters, fragments of broken glass. She looks past scraps of newspaper grasping like hands onto chainlink fencing, past gray buildings and grey sky. She gazes off into the distance. She waits.

Across town in a dimly-lit bar a man sits drinking bloody marys and chain-smoking cigarettes. He stares at a black spot on the floor, studies it, thinks of a woman witing in a playground, her face flushed, her hands trembling.

The woman sits on the edge of a see-saw, lights a cigarette, thinks of a man. She thinks of his hands caressing her ass, his eyes closing, his mouth opening. She thinks of his naked body reflected in a hotel mirror, white flesh searing her thighs, black hair spread across a pillow.

The man stands up, his head swimming with memories of the woman's scent. Her words scrape across his brain like metal fingernails. He remembers her lips brushing his back, her black dress crumpled in a corner, lipstick stains on white sheets. He begins walking toward the playground.

The woman bends down, straightens the seams of her stockings. Silence clings to her ribs. She struggles to remember the man's face, his brown eyes, his lips. She digs her nails into her palm; a single drop of blood falls onto her wrist. She lights another cigarette. The metalic taste of blood stings her tongue.

The man walks, fighting wind, black night, low whispers which creep along his spine. He thinks of the woman's white body spread across a dining-room table, blonde hair spilling into his palm, the sound of naked bodies scraping on wood, red and black flashes lingering in his veins. He begins to walk faster.

The woman is a statue. She lies across the see-saw, her rigid body of stone cracking the rotted wood beneath her. Her black coat blows open, exposing naked white marble. Her glossy eyes stare as the wind scatters the contents of her handbag.

The man begins running, longing to fall into the body of the woman, feel her long fingers in his hair, her warm breath on his neck. He runs, a shdow in a moonless night.

In an empty playground a man opens an abandoned black coat. Inside two red-eyed rats take shelter. The wind stirs up shattered pieces of marble, dollar bills, a photograph of the faces of a man and woman reflected in a hotel mirror.

Seven Photographs

You are standing naked at the foot of the bed. You turn, look out the window, gently parting the white curtains. I am staring at you through a hole in the sheet. My eyes are caressing the curves of your ass, your thighs. The photographer is in the next room.

*

You are sleeping with your arms around me. My eyes are open and fixed on a red point of light in the center of the mirror. It grows larger and larger. It cracks the glass and tries to break through. You open your eyes. A shutter clicks.

*

In the morning we are sitting like statues in a plastic garden. My body is heavy, white, but my eyes are on fire. I am thinking about you standing naked in a doorway, a black silhouette with white shafts of light pouring out of your eyes. Your image freezes in my mind.

*

The next morning you open the door. You are wearing a green robe. Your hair is wild, your eyes sleepy. A man in a black trenchcoat hands you an envelope, then leaves. You place the envelope on your kitchen table.

*

That night I am waiting for you. I am dressed completely in white. I am hiding behind the bedroom door. My hands are throbbing like amputated hearts. My eyes are glass marbles.

*

You walk into the bedroom and I run my hands up and down your smooth white arm. You hear a faint rustle, then walk to the window where you stand naked staring at the moon. I walk up behind you.

*

In the morning I am gone. My cigarette smoke has frozen in a glass on your bedside table. You sit at the kitchen table staring at a white spider climbing the wall. You see the envelope, pick it up, open it slowly. Inside there are seven photographs of you standing naked at the foot of the bed.

Photograph

Sylvia stares at the photographs of dead men, men dressed in business suits, shot, stabbed, poisoned, their glassy eyes staring hard into hers. Her eyes remain fixed on one photograph: a man in a gray suit lies dead on a bedroom floor, his hands are crossed over his chest and his trousers are unzipped. He lies next to a bed of black rumpled sheets. A lipstick-stained cigarette burns in an ashtray on the nightstand.

"What do you think?" Sylvia doesn't hear the question. She is fantasizing about the scene. Robert walks up behind her and gently touches her shoulder. She jumps, a shudder runs through her long thin body.

"I'm sorry." Sylvia laughs nervously, then forces a smile. "These are wonderful." Robert kisses her on the lips and smoothes her long red hair.

"Are you ready to eat?" As they eat dinner, Sylvia is distracted. She keeps pouring wine and lighting cigarettes, but she barely touches her food.

She is thinking of the photograph, it burns in her brain like a fire-edged dagger.

Robert looks at Sylvia's face. He is attracted by the glassy look in her green eyes. He reaches for her hand under the table. He imagines her white body spread across his black sheets. He imagines her red lips encircling his penis.

"Sylvia?"

"Yes?" Sylvia forces a smile. She bites nervously at her fingernails, then shoves a shrimp in her mouth.

"Are you okay?"

"Oh, yes, I'm just a little nervous. This is the first time I've been in your house, you know." Robert pours her more wine. He is moved by her nervousness. He feels a sharp pain in his head, a molten nail being driven into his brain.

"Do you like my work?"

"Oh, very much." The image of the dead man flashes in front of Sylvia's eyes. She shivers.

"Not too macabre for you?" Robert strokes Sylvia's fingers one by one.

"No. I've fascinated . . . Tell me, in the photograph of the man in the gray suit lying on the bedroom floor, how is he supposed to have died?"

Robert smiles. He sees Sylvia standing naked in his bedroom. He sees himself binding her wrists with his leopard-skin scarf. "In my fantasy, he was poisoned by his lover. She laced his champagne with arsenic. She made love to him as he was drinking the champagne."

"Interesting," Sylvia says as she lights a cigarette, her hand trembling.

"Is that your favorite?"

"Oh, yes."

Robert stands and walks behind Sylvia. He begins kissing her lightly on the he neck. He unzips the back of her dress and caresses her back, then showers it with wet kisses.

Sylvia extinguishes her cigarette and turns around to face Robert. She grabs his head and kisses him violently on the mouth, her tongue probing his teeth, the inside of his cheeks. She thrusts her tongue in and out of his mouth. The photograph burns in her body like a hot coal. She tries to drown it out.

Robert leads Sylvia to his bedroom. He lies on top of her on the black bedspread. She feels his erection pressing her belly.

"I've wanted you for so long," Robert whispers.

"Me too." Robert and Sylvia lie entwined in the black silk sheets. Sylvia's long red hair flows across Robert's chest. A single candle burns on the nightstand. Robert lights two cigarettes and gives one to Sylvia.

"Would you like some more wine?" Robert asks as he places Sylvia's thumb in his mouth.

"Yes." Sylvia looks at Robert, her eyes shining. She is still moving in the he depths of his body where broken words, shattered glass, and blinding light envelop her.

Robert stands up and moves toward the kitchen. Sylvia stares at the walls of the bedroom. There are none of Robert's photographs on the walls. She looks at the nightstand and realizes that the photograph was taken here in Robert's bedroom. She shudders, thrilled by the thought.

Robert returns with two glasses of wine. Sylvia sits up and pulls the black sheet over her exposed breasts. "No," Robert whispers, "leave it." He touches her right breast with his wine glass; the nipple hardens. As Robert and Sylvia make love again, Sylvia feels herself sinking into a bottomless sleep. She falls into a cavern made of black velvet where her red dreams flicker on the ceiling.

After Sylvia falls asleep, Robert removes her wine glass from the nightstand. He takes it into the kitchen and rinses it out. He moves back into the bedroom and lights another candle. He removes his leopard-skin scarf from a drawer, then uncovers Sylvia's drugged body and positions it on the bed. He binds her hands with the scarf. Sylvia looks like a beautiful statue, her long red hair flowing across her breasts, her white legs spread, exposing her red cunt. Robert removes a small camera from the closet and begins photographing her. His excitement mounts with each click of the shutter. He climbs on top of her and as he photographs her closed eyelids, he comes on her smooth white belly.

In the morning, Sylvia's head pounds. It hurts her to open her eyes. Robert brings her a cup of coffee. "Too much wine, I'm afraid." Robert kisses her on the forehead. "Stay in bed, darling. I have to go to the studio for a few hours." Sylvia sips her coffee. She buries her face in the sheets and inhales Robert's body scent. She sleeps again. When she awakens, there is a note beside her telling her Robert will be back for dinner. Sylvia sighs, rises, and puts on Robert's black robe. She walks toward the living room. Robert has left fruit and cheese for her on the coffee table. She sits on the couch and begins eating.

Her eyes stray to the photograph. She stands and moves toward it. Again she is captivated by it. She imagines herself there, her body sprawled across the bed, Robert standing at the foot of the bed wearing a gray suit. She crawls to the edge of the bed, unzips his trousers, and takes his cock out. She takes it in her mouth, her tongue caressing and probing. Robert is drinking a glass of champagne. He comes in her mouth and she swallows it, savoring his semen like wine. She lights a cigarette. Robert moves toward her, then falls dead at the side of the bed. She folds his arms across his chest, then leaves, her cigarette burning in the ashtray, a circle of blue smoke spiraling to the ceiling.

Sylvia hears Robert's key in the door. She rushes to the couch and sits down. Robert enters the room carrying a bouquet of white roses. He gives her the roses and kisses her gently on the cheek.

"How are you?"

" I'm okay. I'm sorry I'm not dressed, but I had to sleep again."

"I don't mind. You look nice in my robe." Robert crouches to the floor and kisses Sylvia's feet, ankles, calves. Robert rises. "Let's have dinner. Then I have a surprise." Robert feeds Sylvia swordfish with his fork. Every bite is sensual. He teases her mouth until she throbs between the legs. She reaches for his belt.

"Not yet," he whispers. After they finish eating, Robert leads Sylvia into his bedroom. He asks her to sit in a black leather chair placed in the center of the room. He opens the closet and brings out a man's gray suit.

"Sylvia, would you put this on?" Robert strokes her long red hair.

Sylvia feels her head filling with sharp stones. She thinks of the photograph. "Yes."

Robert leaves the bedroom and closes the door. Sylvia puts on the suit. It fits. It is made for woman's body, she thinks, not a man's. Robert knocks on the door.

"Come in." Robert stares at her, running his fingers through his black hair. He gets a fedora out the closet. "Put this on, tuck your hair up into it." Robert then removes a pair of fishnet stockings from a drawer and a pair of black spike-heeled shoes from the closet. "Put these on."

After Sylvia has finished dressing, Robert places her in the black leather chair. "Sit there, I want to look at you." Sylvia smiles, confused, yet excited. "Don't smile. Look serious. You're a businessman." Sylvia feels her hands begin to shake. She sees herself dead on the floor, her glassy eyes staring into a camera lens. Robert continues to stare at Sylvia. A candle flickers on the nightstand, next to an empty glass ashtray. The sheets are still rumpled from last night's encounter. Robert loosens his tie.

Sylvia becomes increasingly nervous. Finally she bursts out laughing. "Robert, is this a joke?" Robert stares at her incomprehensibly.

"What do you mean? You said it was your favorite." Sylvia's body tightens. Robert lights a cigarette and gives it to her. "Smoke this sensuously, as if it were a penis." Sylvia tries to be sexy, but she is too frightened. Her hands shake at Robert's cold unflinching stare. "Sexy!" He orders, removing his jacket. Sylvia finishes the cigarette and Robert takes it from her, grinds it out on the floor. He lights her another one. She shakes her head, he forces it into her mouth. He removes his shirt and unzips his trousers.

"Suck me in-between drags on the cigarette." Sylvia does this, her whole body trembling, but as she feels Robert's warm penis clamped between her teeth, she becomes exited. She moans softly. She kisses his penis, runs her tongue across it, moves the skin up and down with her mouth. Robert cries out her name as he comes. Sylvia swallows his semen.

Robert strokes her cheek, then fastens his trousers. "Finish your cigarette." Robert goes into the bathroom. Sylvia begins to feel ill. She wants to go into the bathroom and vomit, but Robert has locked himself in. Sylvia throws the cigarette on the carpet and grinds it out. It leaves a black mark on the white carpet. Sylvia notices a number of black marks. Fear rises in her throat. She moves toward the bedroom door. It is locked.

Robert emerges from the bathroom. He is wearing a green silk dress, black lace stockings and black high-heeled shoes. His face is covered heavily with make-up, his lips glisten red. Sylvia freezes against the door.

"All my models are women," he says, moving toward Sylvia. He grabs her by the shoulders and kisses her hard on the mouth, biting her tongue. He pushes her to the mirror and shows her her mouth smeared with blood and lipstick.

Sylvia thinks of the photograph. She sees herself dead on the floor, looking up at Robert, his grotesquely made-up face hovering over her, smearing her neck with sticky red lips.

Robert looks at Sylvia. His eyes are full of tears. Sylvia begins to softly cry. Robert pulls her close to him.

31

"I'm sorry, darling . . . you're so sweet . . . but the cigarettes were laced with arsenic . . . my beautiful Sylvia." Robert leads Sylvia to the side of the bed. He positions her on the floor, unzips her trousers, folds her hands on her chest and kisses her cheek.

Sylvia waits, her green eyes staring at the black ceiling. Robert lights a cigarette and sits on the edge of the bed, crossing and recrossing his stockinged legs.

Blackness

Blackness and a single drop of blood slowly inching across the floor, a blood worm moving closer to my open mouth, my closed eyes. And you showering my thighs with kisses.

When I wake up you're gone. I rise, put on your black pajama top and look at myself in the mirror. Pale and thin, black bags under my green eyes. My hands begin to shake. I get a cigarette out of your jacket pocket.

These dreams come every night and in the morning I'm drained, my veins feel empty, flaccid. I make coffee and begin poring over your manuscripts. I'm your editor. That's my official title, but I'm really your breakable lover, creeping in the corners of your black and white house, lipstick smeared across my face from deep kisses, tongues licking teeth, fingernails piercing flesh.

I read your words, they float like dead objects on the page. I remove them, add them, but my mind is swimming through your body, my eyes peer between ribs, my fingers clutch lungs.

At sundown you return, pale, beautiful in your black turtleneck and black trousers. I walk up to you, caress your cheek, run my finger across your lips, you smile, white teeth, blood-red tongue.

You clutch my arm, tell me I'm too thin. I smile, unfasten your trousers, fall to my knees, but you stop me, kiss me on the head like a child and lead me to the table.

You bring me burgundy and rare steak. You feed me the meat sensuously. You tease my mouth, and the throbbing starts between my legs. I laugh, my mouth smeared with grease and blood and lipstick. You kiss me on the mouth and slide your hands up my skirt. I black out.

Four straight lines of white powder, a black wine glass on the nightstand, a note from you. I cry out for your body in the humid three a.m. bed. I hold your underwear close to my heart.

I am lying on the couch when you return. I struggle to rise, but I'm too weak. I look into your eyes. You begin softly crying. You lay your head on my breasts.

I run my fingers through your hair, flames lick my thighs, but I can't make love to you. I want to slide my thin body on top of you, take you inside me, but all I can do is stroke your long white fingers, your manicured nails. You carry me into the bedroom

A shower of magenta rain pounds on my naked belly. You nudge your penis against my thigh, then enter. I smile, my full white breasts cupped in your hands. You pull my breasts hard, then harder, my body splits in two, exposing organs. You caress the beating heart, then rip out my liver and eat it. Blood and gore drip from your fangs.

I wake up sweating. I am too weak to rise. The cocaine and wine lie untouched on the nightstand. I spend the day fantasizing about your body, your beautiful ass, your full mouth, your black eyes piercing my brain like steel spikes.

It is midnight. You return. You walk softly into the bedroom where, pale, emaciated, I lie naked on black silk. You come close to me, kiss each breast, gently stroke my cunt, then kiss me deep in the mouth. I stroke your black hair as your white fangs plunge into my neck.

Basement

You light a match. Red light covers my head as my eyes slowly open. You crouch down beside me in a corner of the basement. I grab your face, run my fingers up and down the stubble, kiss you, my tongue hungrily probing your mouth. We plunge into a black abyss, hands like tentacles grasping. Hold me tighter, I whisper, and you shoot red stars down my throat.

Then we sit in the dark. Our two cigarettes gleam in the dark like orange cat eyes. We sit close together, our hands touching. When? I ask. You caress my fingers one by one.

You bring my hand close to your mouth, lick the veins, place it in your lap, then sear the flesh with your cigarette. I dig my nails into my palm, feel the blood trickle down my wrist. I gently kiss the top of your head. Soon, you say.

You carry me to a different corner in the basement, cover me with your brown tweed coat. I struggle to see your eyes, but see only faint green sparks dying in the blackness of the room. You leave.

I dream I am caught in a spider web. My naked body struggles to break free, but only becomes more tangled in the sticky thread. You come close to the web. You are dressed all in black with a red rose in your lapel. You remove a box from your pocket. I smile. You caress my ass, then open the box removing a black widow. You shove the spider down my throat and tape my mouth shut. You laugh, disappearing in a wall of gray smoke.

I awaken, feel something crawling on my back, start to scream then stop myself as I recognize your fingers caressing my naked flesh. I smile.

When we emerge from a black pool of foam where skeleton fish break each other in two, I squeeze your hand, bite the thumb until I taste metallic blood. When, I whisper, placing my tongue in your ear, when will you do it?

You draw me close to your body. Soon, you murmur, kissing me until the blackness of the room courses through my veins like new blood. I don't feel you go. When I awaken there's a sharp pain in my side, one of your fangs pierces me, draining my strength.

You don't come. I find my food and water, but you don't come. I struggle to remember the curves of your body, the silky hair, the hot mouth. I am cold. I burn my thighs with a cigarette to keep you alive. I search the room for traces of your body, hair, semen, sweat.

I grow thin. Food is left but I don't eat. I sit in the corner struggling to remember your voice. Soon, you said. I remember the warmth of your hands and long to cut off my cold hands, ice blocks that used to caress you. Without your body to touch they are useless. I will cut them off.

I search for a sharp object, glass, a knife, a razor, a plate. . . I break the plate into pieces, find the biggest sliver and press it to close to my breast. Tomorrow, I whisper as a single drop of blood drips down my chest and onto my belly.

I dream of you. You enfold me in your arms. I am trapped there. I struggle to break free but I can't. Our bodies are growing together. You kiss me and our lips stick together. Our bodies merge, becoming a giant mass of flesh. Our eyes grow together and everything goes black.

Shaking uncontrollably, I awaken in the darkness. My body aches, my head floats, my ribs jut out under the thin flesh. I pick up the sliver.

Then I am swimming in a river of red mouths. My hair catches on jagged yellow teeth. Faceless creatures wait on the shore, holding metal boxes. Each box will hold one part of your body, they say. When they cut out my heart they bring to you and you serve it with scrambled eggs to your faceless lover.

I black out. You open the door. Light floods into the black, dank room. Now, you shout, your face glistening, your body healthy and tan. In the corner you find two severed hands.

After You've Left Me
To Scratch The Walls

A coin drops into a bleeding stream in my heart. It's a tip you've left me after you've left me to scratch the walls until you come back smiling and tan with venom shining on your lips.

These months pass slowly. First I am ice. My body is heavy and cold with jagged edges. Then you send me an ice pick in a manila envelope.

I hold it between my cold fingers like I hold your penis when you are here, but it is steel, not flesh. I stab my arm. Blue liquid slowly trickles out. Then I slit my arm from elbow to wrist. The warm blood drips onto the concrete floor. It flows blue, yellow, then red. I cry ice cubes as I rub my face in the pool of blood which lies at the foot of the bed.

I am pale, drained of blood by your vampire heart. When I stand I faint. My reflection glares at me from a gold-trimmed mirror. I pull out my teeth one by one.

A few days later you send me a black pearl knife. I shred the clothes you left behind. I rip up photographs of you, love letters you've sent full of scrawled sentences which look like snakes ready to bite. In the yellow moonlight which stains my thin body, I puncture my eyes.

Blind, toothless, I sit on the floor reading a book you wanted to write but never did. In it a man and a woman sit like statues at a table. Their bodies are black marble but their hearts glow purple through the stone. They touch hands and the sky splits open and five red doves emerge from the wound.

You send me a postcard. It says nothing. It is blank on the front and the back, but I know it's from you because I smell your body on it, the sweet smell of your neck, your navel, your ass.

Then I am sick for seven days. I vomit up air and feathers. I pull my hair out in clumps. I scream your name, digging my red nails into my thighs until blood runs down to my feet. I drown in a pool of magenta foam. I shatter all the windows with my fist. I burn my wrists with cigarettes.

I am numb. You send me a word which is twisted and ugly, a deformed word ripped from your lungs, a word of mangled flesh and bitter tears. You send this to me but I am numb.

You are here, but like a reflection of a shadow in a hall of mirrors, I can't seem to find you. I struggle to touch you, feel the curves of your body, feel your body stretched out under mine, but I feel only the sharp pain of a needle entering a vein.

You break me open and I bleed white worms onto the bed.

Red Light Story

The light in the window is red. He's put the red bulb in the lamp. That means I can go to his door; it's my turn. When I see red light pouring through his torn lace curtains, my brain falls to pieces. I will go to the door, knock, and he will let me in, then embrace me, kiss me until my mouth bleeds, push me up against the wall, fuck me, then turn me out into the moonless night.

At least that's what he thinks will happen. He thinks I'll be out of sight in five minutes, and he'll put a blue bulb in the lamp. I know. I've been his lover for a year, but tonight will be different.

We met in a room of smoke. He appeared suddenly in the middle of the room, and I watched him brush raven feathers from his red coat. I gave him my silver bracelet. I whispered in his ear during dinner. During the first course I told him we must be together. I told him that when I saw him standing in the middle of the room, my eyes filled with stones. He glanced up from his steak. During dessert, I told him that when we sat so close, drinking each other's breath, I no longer feared death. He laughed and ordered coffee.

Yes, he wanted me, but only for an hour each night. It was better that way, he said. I let him slide his hand in my black silk blouse and gently pull out my heart. He put it in a silver box, then smiled lewdly. He said I should come to his house the next night, the gash should be healed by then. He said my color would be red.

I came, of course. I came with a bandage on my breast. I came smelling of jasmine and cigarette smoke and the damp grass where I had been sleeping since I followed him home the night before.

His house was furnished in black and white. It looked like a chess board where he arranged his lovers like beautiful statues. I looked for traces of the other women, the yellow woman, the blue woman, the white woman, the green woman, but found nothing. The antiseptic smell of the house made me slightly dizzy. His deep kisses and skilled hands made me shiver. Making love with him was like tasting the edges of a wonderful dessert, like glimpsing the shimmering rooftops of a gold city. I wanted to hold him all night, kiss every part of his body, but I had to leave, of course.

He said little that first night, or on any subsequent night. I spoke of the beauty of his body as he lay with his back turned to me. He smoked a cigarette, talked glibly about a painting on the wall, then pushed me out the door. My whole body felt numb. I walked back to my spot in the grass.

Every night with him was the same. He touched my soul with his body, then withdrew into his sterile bathroom to wash me off. My heart breathed inside his silver box and I was left with only a shattered brain.

He never knew that I slept each night outside his house. I watched the other women come and go. He saw five women each night, women whose names he never bothered to learn. He always called me Red.

I thought the others were treated the same. I felt like I was watching myself meet him each hour. My body shook with the pleasure he gave the other four women. On warm nights, he would sometimes open the window, and I could see the shadows of the entwined bodies playing on the wall.

Mornings my hands shook, I had dark purple circles around my eyes, I couldn't remember how to speak. It was as if he had made love to me five times instead of just once.

But last night all the mirrors shattered. I crept close to the bedroom window to spy on my lover and the yellow woman. It was a warm night and the window was open. I could hear them talking. I thought hearing him speak the same words to another woman would increase my pleasure, but I saw him sitting on the bed with his arm around the woman. They were naked and he was speaking very softly to her. His eyes were blazing with tenderness and passion. She had her face turned away from him. He told her he loved her and was trying to find a way to change so they could get married. He was going into therapy, he said. She was crying. He stood up and put on some music. The jazz music shot into my brain like splinters of glass. My lover and the yellow woman started making love. He was smiling and whispering in her ear. He and I had never even had a conversation.

Tonight will be different, though. I have a surprise for him in a black box, a surprise that feels warm against my breasts. After the yellow woman left last night, I followed her. She went to a bar to think about her happiness. I sat down beside her, bought her a drink, caressed her cheek. She was so happy she wanted to make love to me. She said I had sad eyes, a thin body, nervous hands. She said she wanted to give me a night of pleasure and tenderness. And as she was staring at my white throat, I took out a knife.

I see his silhouette behind the torn lace curtains. I am smiling as I knock on the door, the black box pressed close to my right breast.

Your House

You live in a house with open doors and windows. I stand in the center of your house, waiting. Tonight you walk through the front door. You are glistening and naked, and when you touch me, I sprout wings. We sleep in a red room filled with floating feathers. Each kiss is a violet petal flowing through my veins.

Last night you came like a whisper through the wall. You touched my sleeping body and I fell into your arms as into a dream of endless clouds. When you left this morning I could smell you on my body.

Tomorrow you will climb through the front window like a shaft of white light. You will blind me with your face and your glowing fingertips. Our bodies will shimmer like silver fish in a black aquarium as we fall through waves of night.

In the morning we will cover our faces with the sheets. The day will pass like a nightmare of black trees and red lava and we will find each other's hands on the shores of night. Our cries will burst through the ceiling.

But as I stand in the center of your house my hands knot into fists. One night sticks in my throat, then clamps my heart with steel tentacles.

It is late. Red leering faces peer through the curtains. Suddenly you crawl up from the basement. Your skin is green and you carry a sword in each hand. I open my arms, my legs, my mouth, and try to touch your skin, but you unsheathe your swords. You pierce my naked body; my blood stains your white floor. I am bleeding, thrashing, choking on clotted desire. You puncture my eyes and I run stumbling after you, but you are gone.

The wind blows through the open windows and doors.

In a Black Room

A black curtain lies crumpled in the corner. A cigarette burns in a glass ashtray. You enter the room wearing only the blue scarf she gave you. It covers your eyes as you stroke your face, thinking of her. She is gone. A breeze blowing through the open window smells of her body. You sit on the bed and wait.

White hands caressing your back, open mouths, clenched teeth. She opens your chest with a pen knife, removes your heart, places it on her head. Blood drips down her smooth white cheeks. She stares at your open body, probes the organs with long red nails.

You awake sweating, strangling in a twisted white sheet. You reach out for her, grasp cold air that pierces like steel. You light one of her cigarettes, think of her mouth pressed to the small of your back, lipstick smears on your belly.

She slips through your arms, stands at the foot of the bed, staring at your sleeping body, your tired face. She caresses your ankles, kisses your thighs, leaves wrapped in a black cape, dreaming of your hands stroking her hair.

You wait in a pink room. She enters, dark purple circles under her eyes, a hospital gown clinging to her emaciated body. She touches you on the shoulder, falls to her knees, cries out your name.

In a café you draw sketches of her face on a napkin. You see her sprawled across a black table, surrounded by candles, a bride's veil covering her face.

She hands you her shriveled heart. You take it into your mouth. She kisses you roughly, shoving the heart down your throat with her tongue.

You lie next to her, pale, broken, empty sockets blankly staring at a wall. She kisses your neck, sucks your earlobe. You lie still beneath crisp white sheets.

Blood and glass on the kitchen floor. Her body face down on white carpet. Your long fingers tangled in her black hair.

In a black room her photograph stares with deep blue eyes. You sit on the bed and wait.

A Train Enters a Tunnel

While clasping her lover's hand firmly and pressing her thigh next to his, Dorothy looks up and sees her lover sitting at the front of the train car. Her lover's double is staring intently at her. She looks at the man sitting next to her, but he seems to notice nothing. He makes a comment about a man's beard being too bushy. Dorothy buries her head on his shoulder.

She begins caressing her lover's thighs, running her fingers through his hair. She tries to forget about the man sitting at the front of the train car.

"Trains are so sexy," she whispers in her lover's ear. He bites her ear, then kisses her lightly on the lips. Dorothy smiles, pulls him close. "Patrick," she says, "do you think we can do it on the train?"

"We'll find a way," he says while brushing the back of his hand against her left breast. She leans back in her seat, excited by Patrick, lulled by the steady rocking of the train. She takes a compact out of her bag and begins powdering her nose. As she is about to close the lid, she sees her lover's face in the mirror. He's sitting two seats behind her, smiling lewdly, running his long white fingers through his black hair. She reaches out.

No, she thinks, he's sitting next to me, discussing steam engines with a white-haired man in plaid trousers. She closes the compact and forces herself to sleep.

When she awakens the train is coming to a stop. Her lover is smiling at her. He brushes the curly blonde hair from her face and tells her it's time for lunch. She sighs. Perhaps it was a dream.

The dingy cafeteria is crowded with red-faced children and badly-dressed men and women. Dorothy and Patrick line up behind a man in an engineer's cap who looks like a demented Santa Claus. They barely restrain their laughter.

"Isn't the glamour of this trip too, too much?" Patrick asks in an exaggerated British accent. They laugh, then embrace. Dorothy kisses Patrick's cheek and places her head on his shoulder. While they are looking for an empty table, Dorothy sees Patrick's double standing next to the men's bathroom. He beckons to her, his black hair flowing, his eyes smoldering. Dorothy stands hypnotized by his beauty. Santa Claus bumps into her and breaks the trance.

"Dorothy," Patrick asks, "what's wrong? What are you staring at?"

"Nothing." She smiles and moves toward the empty picnic table. Dorothy is unable to eat her lunch. She keeps thinking of Patrick's double, of his beauty. If only I could kiss him hard on the mouth, she thinks.

She looks up from her plate and sees Patrick staring at her. His face seems dull, his eyes seem small and cold. She looks away.

"Dorothy?" "Yes." She can't look Patrick in the eye. She is suddenly revolted by the thought of him touching her. She looks at the gravy he's carelessly spilled on his red shirt and she wants to fling her water glass at him. She stands up and walks away, moving toward the men's bathroom.

Patrick sits still with a confused look on his face. He feels as if she has thrust a shard of glass into his belly. He stands and rushes after her.

She begins to run faster and faster. She rushes inside the men's bathroom and locks the door. Patrick beats furiously on the door. Dorothy begins to laugh hideously.

"You and your dull eyes," she screams, "and your gravy-stained shirt! I want flaming hair and smoldering eyes and flesh I can drown in!"

Patrick tries to speak calmly to her. A crowd has gathered outside the door. Women with beehive hairdos shake their heads disapprovingly and complain to their rotund plaid husbands.

Dorothy sinks to the floor. She closes her eyes. When she opens them she is no longer in the bathroom. She is lying on the floor of a room covered entirely in black leather. She is wearing a black negligee and black fishnet stockings. It is quiet.

She looks around and sees Patrick's double standing in a corner. Dressed entirely in black leather, he seems to be part of the wall. He removes his mask and Dorothy sees flowing hair and shining eyes. She crawls over to him and clasps his knees. Please, she whispers, please. He removes a black whip from his belt and raises it above her. Dorothy closes her eyes.

She awakens to the shrill train whistle. She is sitting close to Patrick in the train car. He is holding her tightly in his arms. He looks at her with sad eyes. She feels a sharp pain in her chest.

"Dorothy," he whispers, stroking her hair, "are you okay.?"

"Yes." She smiles and begins caressing his fingers. He kisses her cheek and holds her gently as if she might shatter at any moment, as if she might be a glass woman. She kisses him on the lips. "Patrick?"

"Yes?" "Do you still want to make love on the train?"

Uncomfortable with her suggestion, he smiles anyway. "Sure, I'd love to. If we go to the back of the train, I know a place."

They both stand and begin moving toward the rear of the train. As they move from car to car, Dorothy notices that the train is ascending a steep hill. Patrick seems dazed and unconcerned about the scenery.

They reach the last car and go outside to the opening behind it. Patrick locks the door. "Here," he says, caressing her ass. Dorothy thrills at the touch of Patrick's warm, soft hands. "Bend over, darling . . . yes, get on your knees . . . there." As Patrick enters her, she cries out in ecstasy. She feels the landscape engulf her. Black trees scratch her face, rocks tumble through her veins. The train enters a tunnel.

Dorothy starts to come. She moans Patrick's name over and over. As the train leaves the tunnel Dorothy looks up at the door of the train car. She sees a face pressed against the glass: Patrick's double is staring intently at her, his eyes glowing red.

Dorothy screams and pulls herself away from Patrick and moves to the edge of the railing. She feels a burning in her chest like a hot poker searing her heart as the double continues to stare at her. .

The train whistle echoes along with Patrick's scream as Dorothy plunges into the gorge.

reflections in my ten red fingernails which I reveal to you one by one

a severed hand crawling
wet along a sidewalk

*

an image in a puddle
faint outlines which
form alternately
your face and her body

*

our underwear lying
in a corner suddenly
catching fire and
burning to ashes

*

my eyes peering through
the ceiling as
she drives a nail
into your forehead

*

our bodies lost
in a tunnel
running frantically
looking for our faces

*

a photograph
of our naked bodies
in an art museum
hanging entwined

*

eyes disembodied
entering
your nipples

*

red lips and
black capes reflected
in endless
halls of mirrors

*

two teardrops
frozen in a vase

Killer

The killer picks up the knife, wipes the blade clean with long, white fingers, leaves the corpse posed on black sheets, posed waiting for a lover, black lace, closed eyes. The killer kisses the dead woman's lips, a drop of blood trickles down his chin.

The killer comes back to you. You lie sleeping on a white sofa. The killer moves toward you, touches your ass, caresses your thighs. You smile through veils of sleep. In your dream the killer pushes you against the wall, fucks you until the suspenders on your garter belt snap, then opens his hand and shows you an open gash in his palm.

The killer carries you to the large white bed where you and the killer swim in each other's flesh, grasping hands, broken sighs, red neon flashes. He takes off your tight wool dress, your lace stockings. He puts you between the sheets. In your dream the killer binds your hands with white lace handkerchiefs that smell of blood.

The killer sits alone in the dark, chain-smoking, thinking of a woman positioned on a bed, a beautiful woman with green eyes and long fuchsia nails. He thinks of his gloved hands touching her cheeks. The killer cries out your name.

But you continue to dream. Elegant severed hands crawling across a lavender table, the killer's tongue probing your mouth, broken glass scattered across a deserted highway.

The killer takes you in his arms, holds your sleeping body close, kisses your eyelids, your breasts, your belly. He unzips his trousers and gently enters you, makes love to you slowly from behind. Through layers of sleep you struggle to remember his face, his hands, the sound of his voice. He comes, then falls on top of your sleeping body.

You awake in his arms, inhaling his breath. You caress the dark purple circles under the killer's eyes, he buries his face in your breasts. While stroking his black hair, you ask him to tell you the woman's name. He whispers in your ear, he whispers your name.

The killer sits alone at a bar, drinking gin, chain-smoking. He inhales his fingers, fingers that smell of your body. He is watching a woman with red hair who sits alone. The woman stands, moves to the bar, brushes up against the killer, smiles, orders a gin, sits down next to him. The killer digs his nails into his palm.

The woman's apartment is pink and white. The killer sits still on an overstuffed pink couch. The woman emerges from the bedroom wearing a sheer black nightgown. The killer stares at a black mark on the ceiling.

The woman leads him into the bedroom pushes him onto the canopied bed. The killer removes black leather gloves from his jacket pocket, puts them on while the woman peels off the nightgown.

Your eye flutters, stares bloodshot through a hole in the wall. The killer stares at your green eye as he strangles the woman. He watches the eye fill with tears. He looks away.

You stand in the doorway wearing the redhead's nightgown. The killer approaches you, strokes your hair, places you on the edge of the white bed. You begin to cry uncontrollably. The killer licks tears from your cheeks.

At dawn you stroke the killer's naked body, tease it, kiss it. As you mount the killer you see yourself reflected in the bedroom mirror, you think of the redhead's body sprawled across the pink canopied bed. You come immediately.

You sit in a café, drinking coffee, thinking of the killer sitting at a bar, staring at a blonde woman wearing red leather dress. The killer comes up behind you, touches you on the shoulder. His eyes are bloodshot, his hands are stained with black blood. He sits next to you, s tares at his reflection in the metal table, kisses you on the lips, leaves.

The killer lies dead on the white bed, his throat slit with a razor. You undress and lie down next to him. Blood smears across your naked flesh. You kiss the killer's eyelids, his mouth. You take the razor from his hand and press it to your lips.

Metal Lover

I know he won't find me if I go far enough into the forest. I can lose myself in the deep red trees, in the blackness which closes around me like a lover's embrace. He'll never find me here when I've swallowed these berries.

I'm sure he doesn't know I'm gone. He's buried in the sheets. I was there with him, holding him close, when suddenly I realized his hands were metal blades and I had to squirm out of his arms carefully or I would be decapitated.

He's been changing lately. Last week I caught a glimpse of him in the bedroom mirror and I swear half of his face had been shredded and was hanging loose and bloody. He must have cut himself with his hands. And Tuesday night when we were making love his penis felt like a knife inside me. I was sure I was being cut to pieces.

He says I'm tired and I'm imagining things, but he's just afraid because I've started to catch on to him. That beast I saw slithering on his tongue has changed him. Every night I try to kill my deep hunger for him so I can leave, even though I'm afraid he has my soul.

Tonight I've escaped him physically. I've burst the vein that's been strangling me. His body is a machine; now I know. I've smashed the memory of his warm human flesh because it no longer exists.

I know he's trying to kill me. He killed a cat Wednesday night, slit it open, and then called it by my name. He took it into the bathroom and locked the door. He thought I couldn't see, but I snuck outside and peered in through the crack in the bathroom curtains. I saw his long knife pierce the cat, spill its heart and entrails on the floor. The cat's white fur turned crimson. Now I know he was rehearsing my death. I know if I stay he'll turn my white body completely red.

Tonight I acted calm and kind so he wouldn't watch me all night like he's been doing. Those eyes on the back of his hand watch me when they think I'm behaving oddly. I think they're electronic eyes with cameras inside them. I was sweet and thoughtful and stroked his hair, even though it's made of metal wires.

I've escaped, but the hole in me is starting ache. I'm afraid it's too late for me to get completely free from him. His wire tubes have sucked out my soul and he keeps it in a black jar where it glows yellow. I've seen it at night when I get out of bed to have a cigarette. He always tells me it's just a reflection of the moon, but I can see very clearly that it is my soul, and I'm afraid I can't get it back.

Maybe these berries will help. He thinks they look like pills, but I know they're berries. I picked them in the forest when we were first in love. I kept them as a reminder of the spot in the forest where we made love and held each other all night.

I remember his warm breath and his silky flesh. Now all that's left are these berries. He is only metal and wire and tentacles now.

I'm sorry he had to change. It was sad to see him lose his skin. The berries are making me very tired. I'll lie down in these leaves. I still remember his hands before they were blades, how they gently stroked me.

Left Hand

As Ren enters the restaurant he pauses to stare at a neon sign flashing WANDA'S. He gazes into the glass door where his reflection appears, disappears, then reappears bathed in pink light. He smoothes his black hair, adjusts his tie, and enters.

He sits at a quiet table in a corner, fingering the wine list, smoking nervously, thinking of the closed eyes of a woman: blue eyepaint, dark lashes. He orders a glass of burgundy and waits for her to tap him on the shoulder with her supple hand.

Ren lights his fifth cigarette while sipping his third glass of wine. He stares at other tables occupied by lovers. He runs his fingers across his cheek, imagining his hand is her hand. He thinks of her naked body reflected in his bedroom mirror. He remembers staring at her reflection while she caressed him, his tired body sprawled beneath black silk sheets.

He stares at his watch. The waiter asks if he will order, but he shakes his head, lights another cigarette. Finishing the glass of wine, Ren begins caressing his thigh. He imagines her long red nails gently scratching his brown tweed trousers. He rises and moves toward the restroom.

Inside, the locks the door behind him and removes a bottle of red nail polish from his jacket pocket. Then he paints the fingernails on his left hand. Once he is interrupted by a drunk man pounding on the bathroom door, but Ren pretends not to hear. He stares at a black mark on the wall, occasionally blowing on the nails, waiting for the polish to dry.

Back at his table, Ren conceals his left hand in his jacket pocket. He orders dinner and a bottle of wine. He smiles at the waiter and at the people who pass by his table. Inside the pocket he moves his fingers sensuously, then gently strokes his leather belt.

After dinner Ren walks home, clasping his left hand firmly in his right, caressing the fingers. Once he pauses to kiss and lick the lacquered nails.

Arriving at his apartment, Ren hurries inside and locks the door. He collapses on the floor and begins massaging his groin with his left hand. He unzips his trousers, removes his penis, teases it with the fingernails, then grasps it firmly.

Closing his eyes, Ren sees the woman leaning over him, her long blonde hair falling across his chest, her lips repeatedly kissing his thighs.

In his candle-lit bedroom Ren, naked beneath black silk sheets, stares at a reflection of the left hand as it lies still on the opposite pillow.

Fuchsia Lips

Steven paints his lips fuchsia, stares at his reflection in the bedroom mirror. He runs his hands over his hips, thrilling at the sensuousness of the tight black skirt pressed close to his small ass. He lights a cigarette, crossing and recrossing his stockinged legs as he gazes at his seductive image in the mirror.

A knock on the front door draws him away from his reflection.

Sylvia steps into the living room, wearing a man's gray flannel suit, a blue necktie, black fishnet stockings, and spike heels. She runs her hand across Steven's ass. He smiles and coyly tugs at her necktie.

They sit at Steven's black marble table drinking red wine out of blue-tinted wine glasses. Steven removes his high-heeled shoe and caresses Sylvia's thigh with his foot. She sits still like a beautiful statue, red hair and blue eyes shimmering in the dimly-lit room.

Sylvia stands and moves behind Steven's chair. She runs her fingers through his long black hair, then turns the chair around to face her.

Steven's erection bulges under the tight black skirt. Sylvia rips off the skirt and black lace panties, kneels, and begins gently licking his penis.

Sylvia leads Steven into the bedroom and removes his blouse and padded bra. She pushes him onto the black bedspread, then removes two black leather sashes from her jacket pocket. She stares at Steven's naked body sprawled across the bed, the erect penis, the heavily made-up eyes, the smeared fuchsia lipstick. She ties his hands to the bedpost and binds his feet together. Steven writhes in ecstasy.

Sylvia removes her trousers and her black lace panties. She mounts Steven. Her blue necktie dangles, teasing his open mouth.

Sylvia rides Steven violently. She watches their bodies in the mirror, her taut hips, his muscular legs. When he begins to cry, shattered by the violence of their encounter, she removes her necktie and gags him.

She pulls herself off his body, puts on her panties and trousers. She lights a cigarette, smiles seductively, then moves close to him, dangling the cigarette above his chest. His eyes shine like wet black stones.

Sylvia grinds the cigarette into Steven's chest.

Desire

You stand framed in a department store window, a white mannequin dressed in black, blonde hair caressing your cheeks, a diamond tie tack glimmering between your teeth. I stand frozen on the wet pavement, my tired eyes searching your face. I press my hand to the glass window. You move closer, press your lips to the glass separating my hot palm from your body.

I wait for you in a café filled with lovers who hold hands while drinking endless cups of coffee. Bloodshot eyes and cigarette smoke enshroud my table like a veil. I sip red wine, write your name on a white sheet of paper, caress the letters one by one.

Dawn arrives and I lie sleepless on black silk sheets, longing to feel your breath on my neck. I remove one of your letters from the bedside table, but the words have evaporated. All that's left is a smear of red lipstick.

The charcoal eyes of prostitutes taunt me as I stumble down alleys following your scent. Last night in a dream I touched you. You smiled, lifted your shirt, exposing a bleeding wound gouged in your side. I caressed it, then sucked my blood-stained fingers.

In a movie theater you sit alone on the front row. I stare at the outline of your head. Wiping sweat from my palms onto an empty seat, I stand, move toward you, my face flushed, my heart bleeding through my thin white blouse. I sit five seats away from you. You don't see me; your eyes shimmer, buried in the naked bodies on the screen. My eyes stare at your wrists, your ankles, the black belt that encircles your waist. I bow my head, inhaling you. When I look up, you're gone. Your silver watch dangles on the edge of the empty seat.

At midnight you come to my bed. Sleepy, I enfold you in my arms, thrust my tongue in your mouth. I fall into a whirlpool of legs and arms and broken sighs. My bones shatter, you glue them back together. My skin breaks open, you pierce me with a needle, stitch it up. In the morning a single strand of your hair is wrapped around my wrist.

Masks

I am paid to find you, paid by a figure wearing a white mask etched with red flowers. I don't know your name. I don't know what you look like. All I know is that you have a glass hand, a wooden leg, and a heart-shaped scar on your left cheek.

I am blindfolded by the masked figure and taken to a party. I stand in a room wallpapered with black velvet, white lamps with red bulbs stand in each corner. Everyone in the room is wearing a mask. Someone shoves a glass of wine in my hand.

I move slowly through the room, sipping red wine. My head feels light. I feel as if I am suspended from the ceiling, watching myself move slowly through the room.

I approach the guests one by one. I stare at a figure, ask it to go to the kitchen with me. The first one I approach agrees.

The kitchen is completely white: white walls, white table, white appliances. In a corner a white cat eats white meat off the white floor.

I ask the guest to remove the mask. I want to see the eyes behind the bull's face which covers the figure's head. The guest does not speak, but slowly removes the mask. Two white eyes devoid of pupils stare at me. My head begins to throb, my hands shake. I leave the kitchen and move back into the masked crowd.

After two more glasses of wine I approach another guest. My eyes are drawn to this figure's solid black mask which resembles the black velvet wallpaper. I ask the figure to remove the mask.

This one, like the first, does not protest, but raises its hands and pulls off the mask. I shatter the wine glass I am holding with my fingers. The face is bloated, oozing water and blood. Its throat has been slashed and the wound opens and closes like a mouth. Fish pour out from between the lips.

I try to open the kitchen door and go outside for air. My head throbs, my hand spurts blood onto the white floor. I pull at the handle, widening the gash in my hand.

Finally the door opens. I rush through it, find myself not outside, but in a beautiful bedroom of turquoise and black. My wound has closed up. I feel sleepy and content. I lie on the feather bed. As I close my eyes, the last image I see is a photograph of you, your heart-shaped scar shimmering, your glass hand clasped firmly on your wooden leg.

When I awaken, I find you lying in bed next to me, your wooden leg pressed close to my thigh. You are beautiful. I lie still, afraid of waking you, afraid of spoiling the silence which shrouds our bodies. I inhale your scent, close my eyes. When I open them you have disappeared. A sliver of glass rests on your pillow.

I get up, search for a door, but find none. I take your photograph off the wall, stare at it. I step into your closet, caress your clothes, undress, put some of them on. I go through your drawers, find traces of your scent, your hair. I long to feel your wooden leg pressed next to me, touch your heart-shaped scar.

As I am sprawled on the bed, positioning myself in the place where you slept, feeling the warmth left by your body, my employer appears, dressed in a black robe, wearing a white lace mask. I stand. The figure hands me a pistol, blindfolds me, orders me to find and kill you.

Now I am in a movie theater. I can't see clearly, shadowy figures crouch beneath seats. The screen is blank. I explore the rows of seats, but find nothing. The theater is deserted.

The screen turns black, a soundtrack crackles. Suddenly you appear on the screen. I sit in a seat and watch you, the pistol clasped firmly in my hand. You are lying on my bed dressed in my clothes. My employer appears and hands you a pistol and tells you to kill me. The figure blindfolds you as the film fades to white.

You are sitting next to me. I feel your glass hand reaching for my flesh one. You press your wooden leg close to me. As my pistol drops to the floor, the crash echoes through the empty theater. The lights go out.

Body

I turn the body over because I recognize the skin. The face has decomposed but I know that my hands have touched that skin. I can see the faint imprint of my fingers on the thighs. I run my fingers through the hair and slowly walk away.

Then I remember. It must be you. That must be your body washed up on the shore, tossed out of the ocean, tangled in seaweed. Your body looks beautiful in the moonlight even though your face is gone. I imagine making love to your faceless body, running my hands up and down your bloated skin, kissing your decaying face.

The waves wash you away and I walk to a restaurant, my mouth still tasting of salt and seaweed. I order a glass of wine. I am lost in images of your face reflected in a bedroom mirror. I can almost hear your voice. I whisper your name and look up at the television screen. I see a black and white movie. A woman is walking on a beach. She sees a dead body washed up on the shore. She turns the body over so she can see the face.

You put your hand on my shoulder. You lead me to a beach where a woman is leaning over a man's body. She turns toward us. She is faceless. You gently undress me. We make love on the sand. I am kissing your chest, caressing your arms.

We sleep with our bodies entwined. I reach up to touch your face, but it's gone. I put my hand through air. I hold onto your body with all my strength, but it turns to sand. When I wake in the morning my body is tangled in seaweed.

Twenty Shores

I

I swallowed you, leaving only
bones and teeth. I buried them
in the garden. Every spring
you sprouted in the yard.

I picked you and kept you in a vase,
but your dead wouldn't go away.
They ascended from shallow graves.
At night you softy called their names.

Then you turned to stone.
I dusted you every day,
and kissed your marble thighs
till you crumbled and blew away.

II

in the broken
dusk
I want to
leave my naked dreams

wrapped in
a package
for you

the thrill
of my head
filling
with stones

III

When the windows open
in your eyes, I look
inside. I see through
the purple glass, the steel curtains.

Ants crawl from the irises,
I see the blue pouring
out of your head, the webs,
the lion's mane that covers your tongue.

I move slowly through the mist
of your body, trying to preserve
the outline, the drunken beating
of your palms.

I memorize
the breathing as
you rise naked out of
cubes of bone.

IV

veins
of a bruised
sky move across
the mirror

laughter rings
out like
coins dropped
on sun-blinded
streets

you sit crouched
in the corner
my naked animal

V

your stitched bone
hands turn
to me caress

the blue lace
of my breasts

jade body
in a web
of rooms

rising in a
magenta fog

broken glass
on a wrist
on your face
on the streets
of my desire

rising in my
throat
in my hips

VI

in the black night
of your bed
my love swells
like a rotting plum
on white flesh

VII

put your hand in the wooden cage
sewn in my arm
and remove the feathers one by one

open the windows in your eyes
and let me swim down your throat
land on your shore

VIII

my lips brush gently
across your silk thighs

your hands slide down
bone ladders of my breasts

we rise together like
birds blinding white horses
with our glittering wings

IX

I saw charcoal bones
pour out of
a train

tears broke
like stones in my palm
the pain of our bodies
froze white in a vase

I heard your round cry
drowning in smoke
dying in the oven
dying entwined with my name

last night I found
your blood on my leg
thin red line
torn from your face

X

I slip my
hand under
the sheet
feel the bones
you leave behind
small skulls
deformed spines

a wind
blows through
the curtains
five bleeding
doves take
flight

XI

The devil
burning in my forehead
the birds
starving in wooden cages
the darts
floating down from the lamps
remind me
that boiling oceans
cough up your divers
on twenty shores

I must hide
a piece of me
in every single
port

XII

glass always
breaks
in my hands
slivers of
a morning
we shared
in another land

on the other side
of the mirror
you stand
stripped
shivering
holding dawn's remains
in your palm

in my house
I am not myself
seeing distorted
faces spread
across the wall
shadows of
your bite

XIII

I dream of a tree with razors
instead of fruit. Every word
that falls from your orange tongue
falls on my palm like a drop of blood

I keep a bouquet of steel
next to your picture. When
your tree sprouts feathers again
I'll fill this mouth with screams

XIV

I see you reflected
in my mirror
I see your mouth
swallowing a sun
swallowing all
the deserts buried in
my soul
your hands reach
through the glass
gently caress
my scars
gently pull
thorns from my wrists
and we melt
two clouds in a
moonless sky

XV

as I am falling
candle wax
sears my
legs

shadows
play in the
back of my
eyes

reflections
of a
blood apple
shattered

hands
shaping my
body

hands
plastering me
to the
black web
ceiling

where you
come
and fuck me
with a
razor blade

XVI

in the basement you
are taking off your clothes
you are sprouting feathers on
your back
you are opening
the surgical bag and
removing the instruments
one by one

I am in the attic
of my heart dressed in the rags
of an angry moon
my fingers glow
then harden into fossils
I am removing the stones
from my eyes
one by one
while you are in
the basement carving
me up

XVII

your fingers grow out of his palms
I know when he slides his hand
up my leg you are touching me

even when your clay statue washes away
even when I pluck your claw
from my breasts you are screaming inside me

I find images of you on his tongue
strands of hair
broken words

clouds swallow him
when I cross the line that leads to a locked door
a blue pulse a raven buried in your arm

XVIII

she must be
slithering
between your
arms tonight

I heard a hiss
in the water
faucet

I saw the blood
ooze
between my legs

her tongue must be
licking
your white bone
thigh

and I must
be a statue
dangling from
a string

a blue
statue
buried
beneath your
eyes

XIX

Once I thought I saw you walking
through sheets of mist. My heart chimed
in its pink steeple, I reached out to you,
but it was only an empty trenchcoat dangling from a pole

That night I dreamed you offered me paradise
but it was too late. White birds
had perched in your skull and
all you could give me was a tattered wing.

XX

I keep seeing your body being devoured
by feathers on a lonely street

the eyes fall out of my madness
I scream

can't you see that I'm
lost blind diseased

a poor beggar tapping at
a window of your dream

Black Hair

I feel his hot breath on my neck, drowning me in his body. But she is in the bed, not me. I can no longer distinguish where her body ends and mine begins. I tremble and cry out as she reaches her climax.

I have been watching them for weeks. I saw them meet in an alley one Saturday evening. I stood pressed against the wall around the corner and watched. She was wearing a green dress and black shoes.

Her long black hair was piled on top of her head in a bun; it unwound beautifully in the hotel room like black crow feathers scattered across the curtains.

I followed them in the bus they took to the hotel. I sat in the back pretending to read a book. He slid his hand up her skirt when he thought no one could see, but I was watching in the mirror. I shivered.

The smell of wheat fields clings to their cries still. I hid myself in a wheat field under the hotel window. The curtains had a gap I could see through. Flashes of flesh and black hair shot out of the room like vertical shafts shooting down my spine. Later, I started seeing her in my mirror.

He never intrigued me. His faded gray suits concealed a body I'd seen many times before, in committee rooms, in all-night cafés. It was her; it was her hair that attracted me. It was hair you could live in, a black forest of trees that completely engulfed him when they made love. They both disappeared and only the erotic movements of the hair remained.

It was always balanced so precariously on her head. One intense look would make it tumble and cover her shoulders. I wanted to run my fingers through it, bury my face in it, feel it flowing up and down my body, hear its dark roar, press it to my lips, bite it, then wrap myself in its silk. Then she moved inside me.

At first I thought I was having a nightmare, but I couldn't wake up. I kept seeing her in the mirror every time I looked, but I couldn't see a face, just tresses of black hair with skin peeping through. My voice started to sound different. I had difficulty controlling my words; her words were slithering up my throat. When I touched my skin I set myself on fire; it was like touching her, like feeling a body wrapped in black hair. I felt I was drowning in black foam. She tumbled out of my dreams at night, fell into the bed, and I thought I had dissolved. I felt trapped under her fingernails.

I couldn't stop watching them. I watched from the wheat field and I could feel her lover on top of me, kissing me, caressing me. After it was over, I'd see a flash of black hair and white breasts between the curtains.

Then I started renting the room after they left. I touched her cigarette butts stained with my red lipstick. I closed my eyes and I could see them so clearly on the bed; I remembered his smell, his hands. I heard myself whispering in her voice. In the mirror I saw a reflection of the two of them making love. I was sandwiched between them.

Gradually, she began bursting through my skin. My body changed, became taller, more slender. I couldn't recognize my voice anymore and I no longer had control of my words. She recited her stories in bars while I was trapped in my ribcage, slowly shriveling up. Then one morning I found a black hair on my pillow.

Then I knew I had to come here today and touch it, feel the black silk on her head. It's as much mine now that she has invaded me. If I could feel it once, I'd gladly sink into her and burn out like the cigarettes she crushes after she's pulled herself from his body.

I am walking up the steps; I know they are here. I can hear them; I can feel him. I'm not going to knock. They left the door open for me. I walk in unnoticed. Her head is sliding under the pillow. Our body is twisted in the sheet. I move toward the bed. My eyes go out.

I am awake on their outlines. My hand is buried in an abandoned head of black hair left on the pillow.

The White Spider

He must cover her with his body or the white spider will touch her. She knows she must lie under his body as under a flesh sheet. That's the only way to keep the spider away. She saw it above the headboard before he turned out the lights, saw it slowly crawling down toward the bed, a white transparent spider.

He falls asleep immediately and begins to snore. She lies awake staring at the small window of the motel room. She hears a dog howl in the distance, sees a black hooded figure move outside the white curtains. She closes her eyes, buries her face in his back, wraps her arms and legs around him, then opens her eyes and stares at the ceiling. This is the last night.

They stopped at this motel two hours ago. Frightened and crying, she said she couldn't drive anymore on the winding wet roads. She said the faces on the tall cliffs kept leering at her. She could hear their faint laughter. Ambulance screams lurked behind every curve of the road. She heard her lover's voice but she couldn't understand what he was saying. Dead deer were strewn on the side of the road. They ran over something on the highway; it felt like a body. Then she stopped the car at a white motel surrounded by darkness and leering cliffs.

It was late and she had to call the manager at his room. She was frightened. Her lover pressed her hand tightly as she made the phone call. All around her she could hear breaking bones, the metallic noises of car accidents. She kissed her lover on the mouth, held him as tight as she could. She was running her hands over his face when the manager walked around the corner. He emerged out of the darkness wearing sandals, his hair wild.

She filled out the registration card, but she couldn't remember her address. She made one up. She couldn't remember if it was Saturday or Sunday. She wasn't sure what state she was in. Locust bugs were buzzing outside, figures moved in the corners of the office. When she turned her head to see them more clearly they hid in the white carpet. She could feel their hearts beating under her feet.

She drove to the room, felt the arms of the cliffs closing around her. She almost screamed at the whiteness of the room when she unlocked the door. Everything in the room was white except for the wooden floor. She wanted to talk, leave all the lights on, watch television, but her lover was tired. He couldn't understand her behavior. She listened to the water beating against his body as he took a shower. She sat still on the white bedspread. It was so quiet she could hear the faces on the cliffs breathing. Her lover came out of the bathroom wearing a white towel, his dark hair slicked back.

She began crying, her body shook violently. He embraced her. They began making love. She ran her hands all over his body, ripped off the towel, saying to herself, this is the last time I'll ever make love, this is the last time I'll taste his mouth, smell his body, feel his weight on top of me and under me . . .

Afterwards, as she lay softly crying in his arms, she saw the spider. She knew that was the sign she had been waiting for. She stopped crying, asked her lover to turn out the lights, and pulled the white sheets and the bedspread over her naked body.

Now she is staring at the window. The black hooded figure is pacing up and down outside. She feels the spider drop onto her pillow. Her lover mumbles in his sleep. She moves her hand up toward the edge of the pillow. The spider crawls onto her wrist. She closes her eyes. Moonlight covers the cliffs like a white sheet. Car brakes screech in the darkness of a sharp corner.

Disappearance

Your body. I find it washed up on a shore. I find it naked and rotting, fish pouring out of the mouth, water glistening on its curves. I find it and press it next to my body, my body grown thin from long nights of looking for you in every corner of every room, digging beneath wooden floors in search of a hair, a shred of clothing, the echo of a word. I find your body and bring it home, keep it in our bed, gently wash it. One day, weeks later, your body turns into a bed of black and red roses. I sleep in the roses which smell of you, petals stick to my thighs, thorns cut my belly.

This is my dream. I've had it every night for two weeks. I've had it ever since you disappeared. I lie in bed, wrapped in a black trenchcoat, a bottle of scotch on the bedside table. I lie here and try to remember your face, the cheeks, the warm mouth, the brown eyes. Then I dream the dream again, the dream where you are dead and rotting and beautiful, the dream where I hold you again in my arms.

I've been searching for you for two weeks. I wear a black trenchcoat with nothing underneath. I wear red high heels, black fishnet gloves. I wear a photograph of you taped to my breasts. I smoke cigarettes one after another. I walk the streets looking in drains, trashcans, restaurants. You elude me, an invisible mist on the edge of a dream.

The first day I was numb. How can a man vanish in the middle of a crowded sidewalk? I felt your smooth hand pressing mine. I stroked it, bent down to kiss it, but before my lips met your white flesh, you had vanished. I stood still. People bumped into me, knocked me down. I kept getting up, looking at the spot where you had been standing. I took lipstick out of my bag and drew a circle around the bit of sidewalk where you had been standing, but I know I circled the wrong place. I knew even then, so soon after you were gone, I couldn't remember the exact spot. My red lipstick smeared across the dirty cement.

I looked for you in department stores, restaurants, banks. I looked for you all night long. At three a.m. I sat in a café, my eyes bloodshot, my hands trembling. I sat and looked into a cold cup of coffee. I thought I saw the shimmer of your teeth in the center of the cup.

Then I went home to our apartment. I fell onto the bed where we used to fall together, hot and wet, drinking each other like flesh brandy. I couldn't sleep. I took a shower and put on your underwear, your sweater. I drank scotch out of your monogrammed glass. I took a sleeping pill and eventually fell into a deep sleep.

First I dreamed I was being attacked by my body. My hands crawled across the floor, dug their nails into my thighs. My feet fell from the ceiling, kicked me in the belly. My ribs floated across a mirrored room, stabbed out my eyes. I was falling into a canyon of spiderweb shadows and broken words. Then I had the dream. Your body. I find it washed upon a shore. I find it naked and rotting.

The next day I went to the police, a photograph of you smiling, wearing a hat, clasped firmly in my hand. I walked into the police station and fell into a sea of gray mouthless faces. I couldn't understand what they were saying to me. I grasped at broken words, phrases. *an. other. how. sex. life. legs. form. pencil.*

Finally, frustrated and confused, I smashed a window in the office with my fist. Glass and blood flew everywhere. I ran out before they could catch me.

Then I showed your photograph to everyone I saw. I went back to the place where you had disappeared and stood there with my eyes closed. I bent down, traces of my lipstick were still visible. I kissed the sidewalk, gently licking it with my tongue.

Then next thing I remember is being driven home in a taxi. This was three days later. I can't remember three days. Sometimes I remember flashes of loud voices, rooms smelling of sweat and sex, clicks of camera shutters, and the dream of your body. I wonder if I found you during those three days, found you and held you, gently stroking your soft black hair, found you and welded you to my body then awoke to find yoiu had turned to smoke, awoke and violently grabbed at ribbons of blue smoke.

When the taxi dropped me off at our apartment I took out my lipstick and wrote on every mirror: 5 days without you.

Two days later I was searching for you in a hall of mirrors. Watching the floor in order to move through the hall, I saw a strand of your black hair. I reached down, picked it up, carefully placed it in my bag. When I went home with a vacuum in my body instead of you, I taped it to the bedroom wall and watched it all night.

The days withered and fell away. The dream began to comfort me. Every night I held your body, your decaying body close to mine. Every night you turned into a bed of roses. Every night I felt you all over me.

Now I lie on our bed in a black trenchcoat. Now our room smells of dust instead of sex. I've had the electricity cut off so I can always be in the dark. I can almost see the outline of your naked body when it's dark, almost reach out and take your hand, press it next to my ass, almost rub my face against your chest.

Tonight I will walk naked to the beach. The seagulls' cries will puncture my flesh like needles. My thin body will shake in the hollow wind. I will walk to the edge of the sea where I will find your body, find it washed up on the shore, find it naked and rotting, fish pouring out of the mouth, water glistening on its curves.

About the Author

CYNTHIA HENDERSHOT was born in New Mexico and now lives in Lubbock, Texas. This is her first book.